This book belongs to...

First Printing, 2020

ISBN 9798675100996

I'm Just Not Sleepy

Anne Underhill

For my darling girl, Edith. Xx

I've had a bath, I've brushed my teeth.
It's time to snuggle underneath,
My comfy duvet with my ted. I wriggle down into my bed.
A hug, a kiss, an "I love you."

"But wait Mum, now I need the loo!"
"Oh no you don't, you went before."
"Mum, please come back, just close the door.
That's too much closed. No that's too wide.
My tummy's got no food inside."

"I'm thirsty Mum, I need a drink!"

"Read a story!"

Once upon a time....

"I want the blue top, not the pink!"

"Mum, tuck me in, my covers wrong!"

"Sing a song!"

La la la...

"Im just not sleepy, can't you see?
I've got a lot more play in me!"

My mum comes in and strokes my head.
She nestles down beside my bed.
"Let's save it up until the morning."

Mum looks sleepy, she keeps yawning.

"Close your eyes and count to ten,
let's count together, ready then?
One, two, three, four,"

Mums gone quiet on the floor...

"Five, six, seven, eight..."

She's dozed off, wow! This is great!

I'll go downstairs, get out of bed.
I'll take my blanket and my ted!

I'll jump

And dance

And sing a song.

I can stay up all night long!

I'll use the couch for bouncing high.
I wonder if the broom can fly.

I'll make a runway down the hall.
Then through the door, above the wall!

Across the sky I'll dive and swoop.
I'll show the bats a loop de loop.

Perhaps they'll join me in my flight.
The owls too! Oh, what a sight!

Out to the ocean with a net,
To catch a whale to be my pet.

I'll keep him in the kitchen sink.
I wonder what he'll eat and drink.
We'll share some milk, a cookie too....

But then I'll flush him down the loo!
That way he can get back to sea.
If I ask nicely, he'll take me.

Perhaps I'll meet a mermaid girl.
She'll show me how to find a pearl.

I'll make a necklace so divine,
The queen will say,
"It must be mine!"

I'll get an invite to the ball!
I'll be the fairest of them all.
I'll dance all night. I'll spin and twirl.
The Prince will gasp "Who is that girl?"

At twelve, when I can dance no more,
I'll dash out of the palace door.
Perhaps I'll leave a shoe behind.....

A treasure for the prince to find!

I'll rush back home before I'm caught,
To all the shopping Mum's just bought!
I'll have a midnight feast for sure!
With **cakes** and **sweets** and **treats** galore!

The smell of sweet treats in the air,
Might lure a MONSTER from his lair......

I'll crouch and wait behind the bin.
Then when he's close,
I'll THROW him in!

But if it turns out he's okay,
I'll let him out so we can play!

Snakes and ladders, pairs and snap.
I bet he'll love my latest app!
I'll tell him jokes to make him smile.
I'll be his best friend by a mile!

I'll have such fun! Stay up so late.
I'm going soon, just have to wait.
I'll stay until I'm really sure.
Perhaps until I hear mum snore.

My eyes feel tired, really dozy,
In my blanket soft and cozy.
Bed feels comfy, I'm so snug.
Teddy's really nice to hug.
A little nap might be just right,
To help me play all through the night.

I finish counting, nine, ten......

Oh no! It's morning time again!

Printed in Great Britain
by Amazon